TAILYPO

A Newfangled Tall Tale

retold by Angela Shelf Medearis

illustrated by Sterling Brown

Holiday House/New York

Now I wasn't there, but I heard this story from someone who was. It seems that a little boy and his momma and daddy lived in an old cabin on a farm in the Texas Hill Country.

Well, this story happened in the hottest part of the summer. Momma and Daddy worked out in the fields until late at night trying to make a cotton crop. They usually left Kennie Ray, their little boy, home alone with his dog, Fang. When that dog was around, Kennie Ray was never afraid. Fang was the roughest, foulest, fiercest, most vicious chihuahua you've ever seen in your life. Some folks said that he was the meanest two-and-a-half pounds of dog flesh in the great state of Texas.

Now, it was Kennie Ray's job to fix breakfast, lunch, and dinner for his parents. Times were hard. For weeks the family had had nothing to eat but beans and greens for breakfast, beans and greens for lunch, and beans and greens for dinner.

Well, one night after dinner, Kennie Ray's momma and daddy got ready to return to the fields to work by moonlight.

"That was a good meal," Momma said.

"Sure was," Daddy said. "But I do wish we had some meat for the pot."

"So do I," Kennie Ray agreed. "There are just enough greens for dinner tonight and breakfast in the morning. We're out of beans."

"We'll be all right," Daddy said as they left for the fields. "Something good will happen. You just wait and see."

Kennie Ray covered the last helping of greens with the heavy iron pot lid. Then he got ready for bed. He'd just settled down with a good book when he heard a strange noise.

Scritch, scritch, scritch. It sounded like it was coming from the porch. Fang started to bark. *Ruff, ruff, ruff, squeak.* Fang's bark wasn't very loud, but you could tell he meant business. Then Kennie Ray heard that sound again. It was louder this time.

Scritch, Scritch, Scritch. It was coming from over near the window. Fang began to leap into the air. He whirled around and around, barking and squeaking.

Well sir, it wasn't long before Kennie Ray heard that sound some more. *SCRITCH, SCRITCH, SCRITCH.* Now, it was real loud. . . . Even worse, something was poking its head into the room. It had two sharp furry ears and slanted yellow eyes like a cat. It had a pointy nose like a rat and long sharp teeth like a lion.

Fang tore off after that critter and began squeaking at it with all his might. Kennie Ray was so scared he didn't know what to do. Then that thing slithered through the window and into the room! It had a scaly body like an alligator and a long, furry tail like a fox. It was the strangest-looking beast Kennie Ray had ever seen.

Quick as a wink, Fang jumped on that creature and sunk his sharp little teeth into its tail. The critter yelled louder than a hog caller at feeding time. It jerked Fang around the room like he was on one of those rides at the county fair in Dallas. Fang hung on for dear life. Then with a flick of its tail, it threw Fang on the bed next to Kennie Ray.

Without a backwards glance, that critter went over to the greens pot and knocked off the lid. Now, greens for breakfast, lunch, and dinner aren't much but they're better than nothing. Kennie Ray and Fang weren't about to let that funny-looking thing eat up their last meal.

Kennie Ray grabbed the broom and commenced to chasing that thing around the cabin. Around and around they went until they were both dizzy. The critter staggered over to the window and tried to crawl out. Just then, Fang leaped up and grabbed its tail again. Well, that critter tried to pull Fang out the window. Kennie Ray grabbed Fang's legs, and with a sharp jerk, he yanked Fang back into the room. They both fell down in a heap. Kennie Ray heard a rapid *scritch, scritch, scritch* as that thing slithered away.

The boy jumped to his feet and slammed all the windows shut. Then he crawled into bed as shaky as a newborn baby calf. Fang leaped up and dropped something next to him. It was long and furry. That critter had shed its tail the way a snake sheds its skin. Kennie Ray put the tail on the mantelpiece. What a night!

Later that evening, Momma and Daddy came home from the fields. Kennie Ray told them all about what had happened. His parents admired the long, soft tail and told their son how proud they were of his quick thinking.

"I'll bet I can take this tail to town and trade it for some groceries," Kennie Ray said.

"I bet you can too," Momma said.

The next morning, Kennie Ray and his parents finished the last of the greens. Momma and Daddy went off to work in the fields. Kennie Ray put the tail into a gunnysack, put the gunnysack into a wagon, and set out for town. Fang followed close behind.

When they got to the store, Kennie Ray sold the tail and bought enough meat and groceries to last the family for months. He even had enough money left over to buy Fang some meaty soup bones. Kennie Ray loaded the groceries in his wagon. Then he and Fang nearly danced all the way home.

It was starting to get dark by the time Kennie Ray and Fang reached the swamp bridge. As they were crossing over, they heard a watery-sounding whisper. It sounded like somebody or something was saying "Tailypo, tailypo, all I want is my tailypo."

The boy and the dog peered down into the water. Two slanted yellow eyes peered up at them. A long nose pointed skyward. A mouth full of sharp white teeth grinned at them evilly. Kennie Ray and Fang ran across that bridge as quickly as they could.

They were out of the woods and near their house when they heard something slithering after them. *Swish, swish, swish.* Two slanted yellow eyes peered out of the woods. Sharp white teeth gleamed in the fading light. Water slid off the critter's scaly body.

"Tailypo, tailypo, all I want is my tailypo," the thing whispered.

Kennie Ray was terrified. Fang began to *grrr-squeak, grrr-squeak, grrr-squeak.* They ran to the cabin as fast as they could go. Breathless, the boy and the dog scooted inside and slammed the door. They were safe, or so they thought.

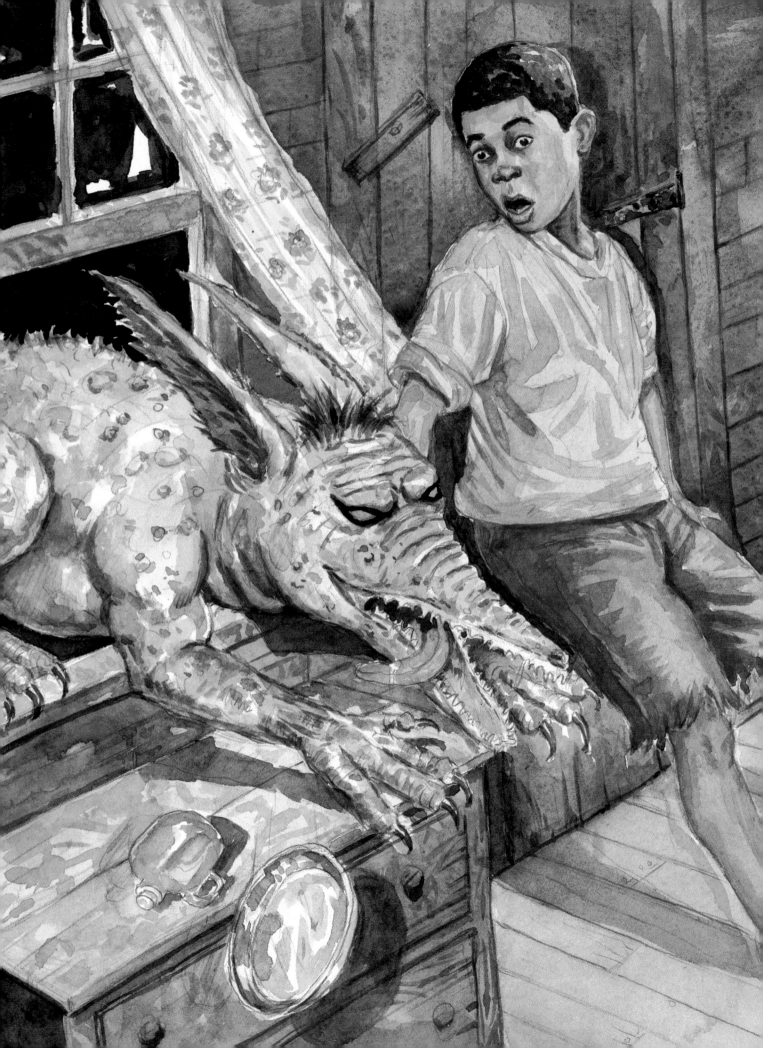

Like a flash of summer lightning, that critter leaped through the window and into the room. Fang tore out after it. Around and around the room they went. Kennie Ray grabbed a broom and joined in the fray. They chased the critter over the furniture and under the furniture. They ran around and around and around until they were all dizzy.

Finally, Fang and Kennie Ray cornered the beast near the fireplace. Suddenly it jumped up onto the mantel. Fang tried to jump after it, but his legs were a mite too short. Fang fell, tumbling right into the empty iron cook pot. That evil critter swung out its paw and knocked the heavy iron lid onto the kettle. Fang couldn't get out!

The critter's sharp white teeth stretched into a grin. It narrowed its yellow eyes and stared at Kennie Ray. Then it began to slowly climb down the side of the fireplace.

The boy was so frightened he didn't know what to do. He leaped into bed and pulled the sheet up under his chin. At the foot of the bed, he saw two furry pointed ears and two yellow slanted eyes. A voice whispered, "Tailypo, tailypo, all I want is my tailypo."

The creature was coming closer! Then its voice whispered a little louder, "Tailypo, tailypo, all I want is my tailypo."

Kennie Ray pulled the sheet up to his eyes. He was trembling from head to toe. The two furry ears, the yellow slanted eyes, the long pointed nose, and the mouthful of sharp white teeth were even closer now. The voice whispered louder,

"Tailypo, tailypo, all I want is my tailypo."

Kennie Ray threw the sheet over his head. He was sure he was done for. Then he heard Fang whimpering in the iron pot. The thought of his poor little dog trapped in that deep dark kettle gave Kennie Ray all the courage he needed. He whipped the sheet off his head and sat up. He found himself and that strange swamp creature staring eyeball to eyeball.

In a loud voice that critter said, "Tailypo, tailypo, all I want is my tailypo!"

Kennie Ray was terrified, but out of nowhere there came a big, huge, horrible voice that roared out of his mouth,

"I DON'T HAVE YOUR TAILYPO!"

Well, that swamp critter was so scared it turned as white as a ghost and rolled head over heels off the bed. It clambered out of the window and disappeared into the dark night.

Kennie Ray jumped out of the bed and slammed down all the windows as fast as he could. He rescued Fang from the iron cook pot and gave him a juicy soup bone. Then, whistling happily, he started to cook dinner.

Soon afterwards, Kennie Ray's momma and daddy came home. Kennie Ray told them all about his adventure while they ate the good food Kennie Ray had prepared. As for that swamp critter, it was never, ever seen again. Well, at least I don't think it ever was.

With love and thanks for all the librarians and teachers who shaped my life and supported
my career, and especially for Becky Buttram, librarian extraordinaire
A.S.M
To my mother, Jewel Brown, and in memory of James Brown.
S.B.

Library of Congress Cataloging-in-Publication Data
Medearis, Angela Shelf, 1956–
Tailypo: a newfangled tall tale/retold by Angela Shelf Medearis;
illustrated by Sterling Brown. — 1st ed.
p.   cm.
Summary: On a farm in the Texas Hill Country, a little boy
confronts a strange critter that tries to steal his family's
last meal.
ISBN 0-8234-1249-0 (hc: alk. paper)
(1. Folklore—United States.)   I. Brown, Sterling, 1963–   ill.
II. Title.
PZ8.1.M468Tai   1996   95-51070   CIP   AC
398.2'0973'01—dc20